The MARCHING BAND MYSTERY

Written by Sharon Peters

Illustrated by Irene Trivas

Troll Associates

Library of Congress Cataloging in Publication Data

Peters, Sharon.
    The marching band mystery.

    Summary: Already late for the big parade, Sheila and
Dixie are horrified to find that their instruments seem
to have disappeared.
    1. Children's stories, American. [1. Parades—
Fiction. 2. Mystery and detective stories] I. Trivas,
Irene, ill. II. Title.
PZ7.P44183Mar   1985   [Fic]   84-8783
ISBN 0-8167-0406-6 (lib. bdg.)
ISBN 0-8167-0407-4 (pbk.)

The MARCHING BAND MYSTERY

Of all the musical instruments in the world to play, I had to pick the accordion. Not that there's anything wrong with the way it sounds, or even the way it looks. The problem is that in order to play an accordion, you have to *wear* it.

And that is why I was not looking forward to the big parade on Main Street. There were going to be colorful balloons and lots of good food. There were going to be baton-twirlers and cheerleaders. The Milburn police and fire-fighters would be marching. And at the mayor's special request, the Milburn School Band would be there, too. So—lucky me—I would get to march for two miles across town carrying my fifty-pound accordion.

There was one other person, however, who was even less excited about the parade. She was my best friend, Dixie Smith. You probably guessed it. She played the tuba.

"Come on, Sheila!" Dixie said on the way
to band practice. "We're going to be late
again. Where were you, anyway?"

"Well, first I couldn't find my uniform," I
explained. "Then I couldn't find my shoes.
And then—"

"Oh, never mind," Dixie said.

I guess that's how Dixie and I became such good friends. We have so much in common. We both play in the school band. We both play unusual instruments. And we are both always late.

"Practice, practice, practice," I complained. "We've had practice every night this week. I wonder if all great musicians had to start out like this. My fingers are getting sore."

"Just wait till after the parade tomorrow and see how your feet feel!" said Dixie.

"You know, sometimes I wish I had learned to play a nice light instrument, like the trumpet or the harmonica," I said. "Then I would be looking forward to the parade, too."

We ran the last few blocks to the school. When we finally arrived, we were out of breath and twenty minutes late.

"Wait," I said. "Let's peek in the window
before we go inside." The band room was in
the basement of the school. We looked in the
small window near the ground. Everyone was
watching Mr. Durkin, the band director,
drawing a map of the parade route on the
chalkboard. Mr. Durkin was proud that our
band was asked to be in the parade. He
wanted us to sound perfect.

"We can sneak in now while he's drawing on the board," I said. We both ran down the stairs to the basement and tiptoed to our seats in the back row.

"Phew! I don't think he saw us," Dixie whispered.

"Maybe he didn't, but I did!" It was Leslie Johnson. She played the flute in front of us. It seemed like Leslie was always there to tell us we were late. Leslie was never late.

"Just don't expect us to wait for you tomorrow," she said. "If you're late—too bad!"

"Oh, Leslie," I said, "go play with your flute."

"Yeah. And may all your notes be sour!" added Dixie.

Just then, Mr. Durkin finished his map and turned to speak to us. "Are there any questions about tomorrow? Please be here promptly at nine o'clock. I'll have a big surprise for all of you when you come to pick up your instruments."

"Easier said than done," I whispered to Dixie.

"What? Being here on time?" she asked.

"No—picking up our instruments," I chuckled. Dixie giggled. That made Leslie turn around again.

"Don't you girls ever pay attention?" she said. "Well, I am not going to let you ruin the parade for everyone. I'll make sure you don't!" Her hair went flying as she spun around in her seat.

"I guess she didn't like my joke," I said to Dixie. "No sense of humor." But I wondered what she meant. I'll admit she had a point about us being late for the parade. It would make things difficult for the rest of the band. I just hoped she didn't try something stupid to prove it.

The rest of band practice went smoothly. We played the national anthem for the ninety-seventh time. And then we practiced "It's a Great Day for a Parade" until I knew every note by heart. I guess all that practice paid off. We really did sound fine! No wonder the mayor wanted us to be in the parade.

I looked over at Dixie. It was fun to watch her. Whenever she played a note, her cheeks puffed out. They looked like they were stuffed with cotton. I'm surprised they ever went back to normal.

Finally, Mr. Durkin said we could stop playing and put away our instruments. I put my accordion in its leather case. Dixie put her tuba in the closet. Just as we were getting ready to leave, Mr. Durkin said we were all invited to his house for a party after the parade. That was the best news I had heard all day.

The day of the parade began like most of my days do—late! After I gobbled down my breakfast, I called Dixie to make sure she was out of bed. I told her to meet me at quarter to nine. I figured that would be enough time for us to get to school. But I didn't figure on Dixie being late.

"You're late!" I said when she finally arrived. "Where were you? It's almost nine o'clock."

"Well," she began, "first, I had to walk the dog. Then I had to feed the cat. And then—"

"Oh, never mind," I said. "We're wasting time. Let's run." Once again, we found ourselves racing to school. And once again, we were late.

It was twenty minutes after nine when we finally got there. "Hey, where is everyone?" I said. The school was empty and silent. There was no sign of Mr. Durkin or the rest of the band.

"I thought he said to meet here," said
Dixie.

"He did," I sighed. "But I'm afraid we're
too late."

"I wonder what the big surprise was,"
Dixie said.

"We'll never know now," I said sadly.

"Wait. I've got an idea," said Dixie. "Let's
see if the door is open. Then we can get our
instruments and try to catch up with them."

"Smart thinking," I said. But when we
tried to open the door it was locked. "Now
what?" I asked.

"I've got it!" she said. "Try the window. If that's open, at least we can get inside."

"What good would that do?" I said. "We'll never get a tuba or an accordion out of that little window."

"No," she said, "but at least we can try to open the door from the inside. Come on, it's our last hope."

For once we were lucky. The window was open. Slowly I let myself drop down into the band room. My feet landed on a desk. "I'm in!" I called to Dixie.

I ran over to the closet and I opened the
door. It was empty. Dixie's tuba was gone! I
looked for my accordion case. It was missing,
too. Where could they be? I went back to the
window to tell Dixie the news.

"What!" she shouted. "How can an accordion and a tuba disappear?"

I thought about it. She was right. They couldn't disappear. But they *could* be stolen. I suggested that to Dixie.

"Stolen? Ridiculous!" she said. "Who in the world would want them?"

I thought some more. Then I knew I had the mystery solved. "Think, Dixie," I said. "Think of someone who wouldn't shed a tear if we missed the parade. Someone who would like to see us in trouble with Mr. Durkin." Dixie still looked confused. So I added, "Think of someone who would like to teach us a lesson about being late." Then Dixie understood.

"Leslie?" she said.

"Of course," I said. "What other answer is there?"

"You really think she would hide our instruments just to keep us out of the parade?" asked Dixie.

"There's only one way to find out," I said. "Let's get right over to the parade and ask her."

"There's one problem," Dixie said. "We don't even know where the band is."

My heart sank. Main Street was two miles long. How would we ever find them? Suddenly, I remembered the map Mr. Durkin drew on the chalkboard. If it was still there, we could figure out where the parade was supposed to begin.

I ran back across the room. Sure enough, the map was still on the board. I studied it carefully. Then I climbed back out of the window.

"Come on," I said. "If we hurry, we can still get there before the parade starts. Then we'll teach that Leslie a lesson. Follow me!"

If I was right, the band would now be at the corner of Main Street and Third. I looked at my watch. The parade would begin in ten minutes. Once again, Dixie and I were trying to beat the clock.

We turned the corner onto Third. There was Mr. Durkin one block up. But where was the band?

"Mr. Durkin! Mr. Durkin!" I yelled. "Wait for us, Mr. Durkin!" Finally, he heard me.

"Mr. Durkin," I gasped, "someone took my accordion!"

"Yeah, and someone stole my tuba," said Dixie.

"Well, well," he said, "look who's here. Now what's all this about missing instruments? They were here just a minute ago."

"*Here?*" I asked. "What are they doing here?"

"There," said Mr. Durkin, "up on the float."

"*Float?* What float?" But as soon as I
asked, I saw it parked nearby. It was a huge
float covered with flowers shaped like musical
instruments. On it hung a large banner that
said "Milburn School Band." Sitting on the
float were all the members of the band.

"That was the big surprise I mentioned," he said. "When you girls weren't at the school by nine-fifteen, I was sure you weren't coming. But Leslie seemed sure that you would just be late. She suggested we bring your instruments along just in case. Now I'm glad we did. If you hurry, you can still take your places on the float."

"You mean we'll be riding the whole time?" asked Dixie.

"Absolutely," said Mr. Durkin. "You didn't think I was going to let you *walk* for two miles carrying those heavy instruments?" He smiled.

I didn't think it was so funny. But I did know that if it hadn't been for Leslie, my accordion and Dixie's tuba would still be locked in the school.

We climbed up on the float and took our seats behind Leslie. "Welcome aboard," she said, and smiled.

"Thanks a lot," I said.

"Yeah. Thanks, Leslie," said Dixie.

The parade was wonderful. Balloons and banners filled the sky. The streets were lined with waving and cheering people. Leslie and Dixie and I played out hearts out. And the Milburn School Band sounded better than ever!

Afterward, we all went over to Mr.
Durkin's for a party. There was plenty of cake
and cookies and ice cream. And do you know
what? Dixie and I made sure we were right on
time!